TUNDRA
the Arctic Land

TUNDRA

by Bruce

Atheneum   1 9

the Arctic Land

Hiscock

8   6   *New York*

Library of Congress Cataloging-in-Publication Data

Hiscock, Bruce.   Tundra, the Arctic land.

Includes index.
SUMMARY: Describes the geography of the tundra and
the animals, plants, birds, and people who have adapted
to life on these arctic plains.
1. Tundra ecology—Juvenile literature.   2. Tundras
—Juvenile literature.   [1. Tundras.   2. Tundra
ecology.   3. Ecology]   I. Title.
QH541.5.T8H57   1986   574.5'2644   85-28769
ISBN 0-689-31219-0

Published simultaneously in Canada by
Collier Macmillan Canada, Inc.
Type set by Linoprint Composition, New York City
Printed and bound by
Fairfield Graphics, Fairfield, Pennsylvania
Layouts by Bruce Hiscock/typography by Mary Ahern
First Edition

to Julia and Frederick

Contents

TUNDRA
the Arctic Land

Chapter 1

Winter Scenes

AT THE TOP of a small hill on the tundra an Arctic ground squirrel stopped and sniffed the wind. It was a blustery day in September, and the ground squirrel's whiskers quivered in the gusts of cold air. The wind smelled of snow, but it smelled clean and safe. There was no scent of fox or wolf nearby. Cautiously, the ground squirrel sat up and looked around. It inspected the rocks and lichens covering the hill and then looked out across the tundra. The ground squirrel could see a long way, for there was not a single tree to block its view.

A series of broad, marshy meadows stretched out from the ground squirrel's hill. The meadows were dotted with small lakes and ponds. Low, stony hills ran through the meadows, dividing them and breaking up the flatness of the land. A few weeks ago the meadows were green and bright. Now they had turned brown, and the wind tugged at the clumps of dry grass. In the dis-

tance the ground sloped up into a long ridge. During the
night the dark ridge had been dusted white with a covering of snow. Only a patch of dwarf spruce remained
green.

The ground squirrel looked carefully at everything,
but it saw no animals moving.

Even the Canada geese that had nested by the lakes
were gone now. One cold morning when the water was
covered with a thin layer of ice, they rose into the air
forming a great vee-shaped pattern against the sky. The
geese had circled the hill and then headed south, honk-
ing noisily.

Since then the skies above the tundra had been gray

and empty. No ravens or owls had been seen for several days.

The ground squirrel looked around once more and then went back to gathering seeds. Big flakes of wet snow began to fall. A flock of ptarmigan cackled faintly from a distant hill. The animal paid no attention to these things. When its cheeks were stuffed with seeds, the ground squirrel hurried down the hill and disappeared into a burrow in the sandy soil.

As the autumn days passed, the ground squirrel continued to eat and collect seeds. Beneath its tan fur a thick layer of fat was forming. The time of hibernation was drawing near.

One morning in early October, the ground squirrel emerged to find the earth frozen hard and a cold, dry snow blowing across the tundra. Already the wind was building little drifts behind each rock on the hill. The ground squirrel blinked the flakes away and twitched its tail.

Suddenly there was a slight vibration, a rumbling in the ground. At the top of the hill a thousand antlered heads appeared. The caribou were coming, migrating toward their winter feeding grounds. The herd trotted quickly down the slope and out onto the meadow. They made a clicking sound as they passed. The caribou streamed across the frozen tundra, and then the main body of the herd was lost from sight as they went up and over another hill.

It began snowing harder as the wind picked up its pace. Out in the meadow a few straggling caribou were running, trying to catch up with the herd. Tiny white flakes clung to their gray fur. In the growing storm two pale wolves began to close in on a caribou that was limping badly. The ground squirrel ducked back into its burrow as the wolves and caribou vanished in a thick swirl of white.

Underground, the animal crept down a long tunnel to a chamber lined with grass. It munched a few seeds and curled up in its nest. The ground squirrel would not see the meadows and sky again until spring. Hibernation had begun.

All around the top of the world, ground squirrels seek their burrows when the cold and snow come to the tundra. This is the land of the far north, the open land beyond the trees. There, winter is the long season, and it begins very early.

By October, the tundra is covered with snow. The days are short and the sun stays low in the sky. Each day it shines a little less and each day the air grows colder. As winter deepens, the days become so short that the sun just flickers above the horizon before it sets again.

Finally, over much of the tundra, the time comes when the sun does not rise at all.

In the darkness the sky is often clear. Northern lights shine overhead and the big dipper makes circle after circle around the north star. On the ground, the wind packs the snow into hard drifts, creating strange sculptured shapes. The hilltops, however, are bare. The wind strips the snow from the high places and sends it rushing across the flat lands like wisps of smoke. Hardly any new snow falls in the coldest part of winter for the air is very dry. Underneath the drifts, hardy plants lie frozen, waiting for the sun to return.

Yet even in the dark of winter there is life on the tundra. A herd of muskoxen roams a ridge, looking for plants exposed by the wind. Their long coats swish about their ankles.

At the edge of a bog, lemmings are busy in a network of tunnels beneath the snow. Dozens of these small, furry creatures move about, nibbling on the roots and stems of plants. Not far away an Arctic fox trots silently on the surface of the snow. A thick white coat protects it from the cold, but the fox is hungry, for the hunting has been poor.

As the fox approaches the bog, it stops, sensing the hidden lemmings close by. The fox moves slowly forward, then suddenly rears up and pounces, breaking through the crust into the lemming's runway. With flashing feet the fox digs along the tunnel, biting and scratching, while a lemming scurries ahead. This time the fox is lucky, and it kills the lemming with one clean snap of its jaws. The fox finishes its meal and, satisfied for now, moves off into the night. The snow sparkles brightly beneath the starlit sky.

There are other kinds of life on the winter tundra as well. Near the Arctic coast a cluster of small houses stands out against the treeless landscape. From each chimney a thin plume of smoke rises in the cold air. Electric lights brighten the windows of every house, casting yellow patterns across the snow. Behind one house a husky dog lies sleeping, curled tightly against the cold. From across the tundra comes the whine of snowmobiles. The dog wakes and pulls at its chain. A father and his sons are returning from their traplines far out on the land. They are bringing home the carcasses of a dozen Arctic fox. As they pass the village store, a group of boys and girls wearing parkas and jeans come out to admire the catch.

In another place on the tundra a different sort of hunter is at work. Bright floodlights chase away the darkness and bulldozers scrape the frozen ground. In a cleared area a crew of men and women begin erecting a drilling rig. These hunters are searching for oil beneath the tundra. They are dressed in heavy clothing and the work goes slowly in the cold.

Men and animals alike face a long, bitterly cold winter on the tundra. The season begins with the first snows of September and lasts until sometime in May. During the coldest months the temperature remains far below zero and the chill wind can be felt through the thickest parka or fur. The Arctic climate has kept the tundra isolated for centuries. Most of the land remains a vast wilderness, untouched and beautiful, where animals wander as they choose. But as the oil and minerals of the warmer lands are used up, development is moving northward despite the Arctic cold.

Chapter 2

The Land Without Trees

TUNDRA covers the northernmost land in the world. It is a treeless, rolling plain that spreads across the top of each continent surrounding the Arctic Ocean. The tundra begins wherever the taiga, the great forests of the north, ends. From there it continues to the Arctic Coast and the islands offshore, forming a broken circle of tundra around the top of the world.

The map on the opposite page shows the tundra in a view of the earth looking down on the North Pole. There is no land at the pole, only the pack ice of the Arctic Ocean. In Europe the band of tundra is narrow, but in Siberia it broadens as it stretches across Asia. Tundra covers much of the coast of Alaska, and in Canada it reaches below the Arctic Circle deep into North America.

The Arctic Circle is an imaginary line that marks the beginning of the land of the midnight sun. At the Arctic Circle there is one day in June when the sun never sets and one day in December when it never rises. Going north from the Arctic Circle the number of days of twenty-four hour sunlight in summer (and total darkness in winter) gradually increases until at the North Pole there is continuous sunlight for half the year.

One of the largest expanses of tundra is just west of Hudson Bay in Canada. This area is called the barren lands and it is one of the least settled regions on Earth. I traveled on the barren lands one summer. Many of the illustrations in this book are based on drawings I did there.

I first saw the tundra when I was eleven years old and we moved to an island off the coast of Alaska. No trees grew there, only a coarse, grassy groundcover. I spent many hours exploring the hills and grew to like the wide open feeling of the land. It was a small island, however, and quite different from the tundra of the far north.

On the barren lands the Arctic tundra is immense and unbroken. This is an area about as big as the Midwestern United States, but it is a wilderness without roads, towns, or stores. All traveling on the barren lands must be done by water or air. Only a handful of people go there each year.

One does not travel on the tundra alone or without careful preparations. I went with an experienced guide, Alex Hall, and a small group of men and women.

The trip to the barren lands left from Fort Smith in the Northwest Territories, and I reached this small village by bus from Edmonton, Alberta.

My bus left Edmonton at midnight. All night long we rolled north through wheatfields and prairies. By morning the woods had begun. Gradually the fields were replaced by trees until there was nothing left but the huge forest of the taiga. The trees were mostly spruce, tall and very pointed. They extended in all directions as far as one could see. The bus became emptier as we went on, and by afternoon the pavement ended and the road changed to gravel.

It took two days of riding through the taiga to reach Fort Smith. The view out the window seldom varied except when we passed through burned over areas. At Fort Smith the road ended and I was the only passenger left on the bus.

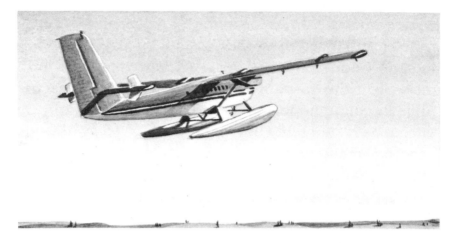

A day later, on a sparkling July morning, the ten members of our group piled into a Twin Otter float plane and took off for the tundra. There was just enough room for all of us and our gear. I sat in a canvas seat by the window and watched the forest far below. After flying for an hour the trees began to thin.

Maps of the Arctic usually show a treeline, where the taiga ends and the tundra begins. The treeline, however, is just a guide, for there is no abrupt end to the forest.

Going north, the trees become smaller and farther apart, until, on the tundra, only an occasional dwarf spruce remains.

We continued flying for another hour. Then the plane banked sharply and landed on a clear, blue lake. The air outside was cool, but the sun was brilliant in the Arctic sky. We carried our gear down the pontoons of the plane and stacked it on the beach.

The pilot refueled his plane from drums he had cached on the shore and took off. We were suddenly alone on the empty land. For the next three weeks we would see no one else.

From the air the tundra looks like a giant golf course splattered with lakes, but up close it is rough and uneven. The hills are crowned with jumbles of stones of all shapes and sizes called fellfields. Below the hills the land is level and wet. There, grass grows in lumpy tussocks and ponds shimmer in the breeze. On the hillsides, dwarf birch and mats of green plants grow close to the ground. Here and there a few small spruce stand upright.

This is how the tundra begins just north of the treeline. From there the pattern is repeated over and over: rock-strewn hills and boggy meadows alternate with thousands of lakes and ponds. The only highways are the big rivers flowing north to the sea.

In Canada, the tundra ends in the islands of the high Arctic above the barren lands. There, as one goes north, the plants and grasses gradually disappear until only lichens are left. This region is sometimes called the polar desert for it is very dry and very cold. Beyond the polar desert, all life on land ceases and there is only ice and rock.

In other parts of the world the Arctic lands look much the same except some are mountainous.

The lack of trees gives the tundra a stark, bare appearance. The shape of each hill stands out clearly. The view seems to go on forever, but without trees, distances are difficult to judge.

Why do trees grow in the taiga, but not on the tundra? There is no simple answer to this question, for many factors are involved. Cold, particularly in summer, inhibits the growth of trees on the tundra, but wind and permafrost also play a role.

Northern trees can survive very cold winters. In fact the coldest temperatures in Siberia and North America always occur in the taiga. There, away from the warming effect of the ocean, the thermometer may dip to –70° C (–94° F). Spruce and tamarack trees endure the winter by remaining largely dormant. When the warm weather returns, they begin growing again. The summer growing season is critical for trees. In the taiga, summers are quite a bit warmer and longer than on the tundra.

Summer on the tundra lasts only about two months. It begins in late June as the lingering snowbanks melt. By the end of August, freezing weather has returned. It is a cool summer as well. In July, the warmest month, the average temperature is about 10° C (50° F) near the tree-line. Further north it is colder still. With a short, cool growing season like this, trees cannot survive. The few that do live seldom get very tall.

I cut down a dead spruce in the barren lands that was only half as high as my knee. With a magnifying glass I counted the growth rings inside the trunk to find out how old the tree was. The trunk was only as thick as my finger, but there were over fifty rings, one for each year the tree had lived.

Wind is also hard on trees, and the tundra is a windy place. Low plants escape the constant battering and twisting that even small trees receive. The larger trees that do live in isolated spots in the southern tundra, grow best where they are sheltered from the wind.

Nearly all of the Arctic tundra (and large sections of the taiga) rests on permafrost. Permafrost is ground that stays frozen all year long. Beneath the tundra, permafrost may extend down for hundreds of meters. In some places in Siberia it is 1.5 kilometers (0.93 miles) deep.

In winter, the tundra freezes solid from the surface on down, but when the spring sun warms the land, the top part of the soil thaws. This creates an "active layer" of moist soil where the tundra plants grow. The active layer is quite shallow in the Arctic and this also discourages trees. Roots cannot grow below the active layer and a tree must have deep roots to stand up against the wind.

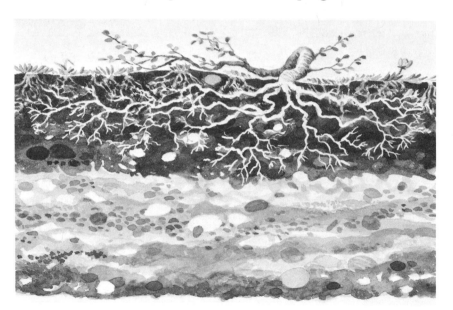

Walking on the tundra in July, it was hard to believe there was permafrost not far beneath my feet. The surface of the ground felt warm, and flowers were blooming everywhere. Just how deep was this active layer? With a strong stick I began probing for permafrost. First I pushed the stick into a patch of wet sand. About a meter down the sand was still soft. I tried again a few steps away, this time choosing a spot that was covered by a thick layer of moss. The stick went in only a little way before it struck something hard. Perhaps it was just a rock. I wiggled the stick around until it had made a hole big enough to slide my arm into. Halfway to my elbow, my fingers touched bottom. The bottom was dirt, frozen hard and icy cold. It was the top of the permafrost layer.

Permafrost is very important to the whole makeup of the tundra because it prevents water from seeping away through the soil. Without permafrost the tundra would look like a desert, for the climate is surprisingly dry.

Most of this area receives less than 25 centimeters (9.8 inches) of precipitation a year, half as rain and half as snow. This is about the same amount of water that falls on a desert each year. In the high Arctic the climate is even drier.

Despite the long months of Arctic cold the tundra is not buried under deep snow each winter. Snow comes and it stays, but it doesn't fall in great amounts. In order

from the intense winter cold. This leaves a series of cracks in the earth similar to those of a dried up mud puddle, except on a larger scale. The cracks eventually fill with water and freeze. The freezing expands the water, pushing up small ridges of soil where plants grow thickly. These polygons are visible from the air, but the shapes are hard to see at ground level.

In other places the frost action is even more dramatic. I was slogging across a long flat section of tundra, looking for caribou, when I saw a perfectly formed round hill rising in the distance. This is a *pingo.* "Pingo" is an Eskimo word meaning round hill.

A pingo is actually a great dome of ice formed by a dying lake. As permafrost surrounds the lake, the water freezes, expanding upward to make the dome. Over hundreds of years the dome becomes covered with dirt and plants until it looks just like a hill of solid ground. If the insulating layer of soil is damaged, however, the ice will begin melting and the pingo will eventually disappear.

Tundra circles are also caused by the cold. Plants cover most of the ground on the tundra, but every so often there are small round areas of bare, sandy soil, usually less than a meter across. These are tundra circles. The soil is often damp and the circle appears to be oozing from the ground. This is exactly the case, for tundra circles are formed by frost pressure forcing plugs of wet soil upward. They are good places to look for animal tracks.

Eskers are also good places to find animal tracks, for wolves like to den in these big sand hills. Eskers are the sandy deposits of rivers that once flowed beneath the glaciers of the ice age. They are long ridges that may wind across the tundra for many kilometers and stand high above the land. Hiking on an esker is like walking along a huge sand dune planted with clumps of trees.

As we canoed on the barren land rivers, we sometimes camped at the base of an esker. Trees grow fairly well in the shelter of eskers, even above the treeline, and there was always dead wood at these sites for fires. Wood is scarce on the tundra, and we were careful to use only what we needed. We usually cooked with wood, saving our gas campstove for emergencies, but we made no late evening campfires. They weren't really necessary, for the sun did not set until shortly before midnight. Although we were south of the Arctic Circle, it was never dark. A bright twilight lasted from sunset until dawn, a few hours later. In my tent at night, I tied a blue bandanna over my eyes when I slept.

WHILE MOST of the world's tundra is in the Arctic, isolated patches of tundra also exist on the tops of high mountains. There, above the timberline, the climate is windy and cold like that of the Far North. A kind of tundra, called alpine tundra, exists in these places. It contains many plants that are similar or identical to those of the Arctic.

Alpine tundra may be found on high mountains almost anywhere in the world. It appears on peaks in the Northeastern United States as well as the Alps, Rockies, and Himalayas. There is a large area of alpine tundra in Rocky Mountain National Park in Colorado that can be reached by car. There visitors can see fellfields and tundra flowers.

These are mountain places, however, with a completely different feeling from the open tundra plains of the Arctic.

plants will grow in the long hours of daylight, making leaves, roots, berries, and seeds. Then the ground will freeze again and summer will be over.

Only a few plants can live under these conditions. The growing season is too short and the air and soil too cool for tomatoes or petunias to survive, but the tundra plants have adapted to the Arctic climate. They have done this in several ways. Most are small plants growing low to the ground. They are very efficient at gathering and storing energy from the sun, even at cool temperatures. They are plants that are able to withstand drought, wind, and cold. Some are so perfectly adapted to the Arctic that they cannot survive in a warmer climate. Others, including lichens, grow elsewhere in the world as well.

Lichens are the very soul of the tundra plant community. About twenty-five hundred kinds can be found in the Arctic growing on the stony soils and the bare surfaces of rocks, or anywhere else that is dry.

These simple and unusual plants have no leaves, roots, stems or flowers. Some look like like tiny cups or

trumpets, other lichens, living on rocks, look like splotches of peeling paint. Lichens are often pale green, but they can be bright orange, red, black or other colors.

Caribou lichens, sometimes called reindeer moss, resemble plastic pot scrubbers or miniature sets of antlers. In places, the ground of the tundra appears speckled because it is covered by brown and white caribou lichens. The lichens are brittle and crisp underfoot when they are dry, but after a rain, they swell and become soft. These lichens are the main food of the caribou, but almost no other animal will eat them.

Lichens are actually two plants, an alga and a fungus, living together. The relationship is beneficial to each partner. The alga, a green plant like pond scum, makes the food. The fungus, which is related to mushrooms, cannot manufacture its own food. It provides a tough, protective covering for the alga and helps store water. Together, as a lichen, they can live in places, such as on rocks in the polar desert, where neither plant could exist alone.

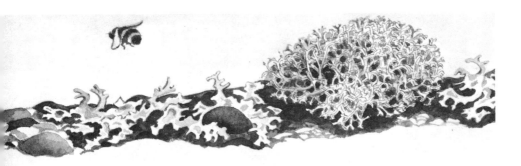

Lichens are particularly well adapted to the Arctic. They can survive long periods of drought and extreme cold and then begin growing again as soon as there is a little moisture and warmth. Of course, they do not grow very fast under these conditions. A lichen as big as your hand may be hundreds of years old. The oldest lichens are five thousand years old. It is only because there are so many lichens on the tundra that these slow-growing plants can provide enough food for the caribou herds.

Where it is too wet for lichens to grow on the tundra, the mosses take over. The damp hollows and the land around the marshes are filled with these soft, springy plants. Mosses are more advanced than lichens, but they are still very simple plants and have no true roots, leaves, or flowers.

Sphagnum moss is common in bogs throughout the North. This is the same moss that is sometimes used in greenhouses to keep hanging plant baskets moist. It is so absorbant that Eskimo mothers once used dried

sphagnum moss in place of diapers. Since Eskimo babies spent much of the day riding in the back of their mother's parka, a good diaper substitute was important. As I walked on the barren lands, my feet told me when I was crossing a patch of sphagnum moss. Most of the tundra is firm, but sphagnum beds are like stepping on a foam mattress.

Along with the mosses, a number of different grasses grow in the wet lands of the tundra, creating beautiful green meadows. The Arctic cotton grass is easy to recognize. It has a delicate white puff at the top of each slender stem. The grasses are not very tall and from a distance the meadows look smooth, dry, and easy to walk on. Up close, however, they are wet and bumpy. The grass grows in hummocks that are ankle-twisters for people. Caribou, though, don't seem to mind the rough ground. They are so surefooted, they just splash across the meadows without looking down.

By early July, the flowers of the tundra are in full bloom. There are fields of yellow Arctic poppies, along with purple monkshood, blue lupines, pink Lapland rosebay, and many others. For a time they provide a spectacular show.

Throughout the summer the hillsides are kept green by small heather plants like bearberry, crowberry, mountain cranberry, and Labrador tea. Along with lichens, they are the most common plants on the tundra.

Bearberry

Crowberry

Mountain Cranberry

The three berries, bearberry, crowberry, and mountain cranberry, are good examples of how plants have adapted to the tundra climate. These plants are very compact. Their leaves are small and leathery to conserve moisture, but they are rich in chlorophyll, the green substance plants use to make food. As the plants grow,

they spread outward (instead of getting taller) eventually forming dense mats of leaves and stems. These mats act as solar collectors, warming the air around the plant. On a sunny day the air next to the plant may be 10 to 15° C (18 to 27° F) warmer than the air above the surface. The warmth allows the plant to grow faster.

Tundra plants collect energy efficiently, and part of this energy is stored for later use. As the plant makes starch and other carbohydrates during the summer, these foods are sent to the roots. The root system of a tundra plant is often several times as large as the plant above ground. The roots do not go very deep though, for they must stay in the active layer. Little of the stored energy is needed during the long winter when the plant is dormant. As spring arrives, the plant uses the food in its roots to send up new leaves and blossoms as quickly as possible. In this way a plant can take full advantage of the short growing season.

Many tundra plants reproduce mainly by sending out runners, which take root and develop into new plants. Flowering plants may grow runners, but they also produce seeds. Seeds, unlike runners, can travel long distances by blowing across the snow or being carried by birds. Because of this, many of the same plants are found on all sides of the Arctic Ocean.

To create a seed, a plant must go through several steps. First a bud is formed, then a flower, then a fruit, and finally the seeds in the fruit must have time to ripen.

The Arctic poppy, like a pea or pumpkin planted in a garden, does this in a single summer, but for many tundra plants the summer is too short. Instead, a seed may require several seasons to develop. A bud produced one summer may lie beneath the snow all winter. It will bloom early the next summer, but another growing season may pass before the seeds are mature.

TUNDRA PLANTS provide the food for tundra animals.

Ground squirrels and lemmings eat seeds and shoots. Caribou graze on lichens and grasses. Muskoxen eat willow and other small plants.

These plant-eating animals are then eaten themselves by the wolf, fox, and owl. This is the food chain of the tundra.

In most climates people eat foods from all parts of the food chain, including plants and animals. The early people of the Arctic, however, lived almost entirely on meat and fat. They hunted caribou and muskox, and also whale, seal, and walrus. They ate very few plants because few tundra plants are edible for humans.

In the barren lands, we carried all our own food. Each of the five canoes had two heavy, plastic-lined packs filled with tea, oatmeal, flour, peanut butter, jam, honey, chocolate bars, raisins and nuts, tins of meat, and many freeze-dried soups and stews. This simple, nourishing fare provided the energy we needed for long days of paddling and portaging. The only foods we took from the land were fish and berries.

The fishing on the tundra is very good. Since few people travel there, most of the fish have never seen a line or a lure. Often, we caught big lake trout or grayling with every cast. Fish fillets, wrapped in foil and cooked over the coals, were a welcome change from our packaged foods.

Berries are one of the few plant foods people can eat on the tundra. Bearberry, crowberry, and cranberry are edible, but not very tasty. Bilberry, a kind of blueberry that grows on the hills, is much better. The bilberry plants we found were small, often no more than ankle high. Still they produced a good crop of berries. We ate the berries on cereal or baked in bannock, a biscuit-like bread that is traditional in the north.

Cloudberries are the favorite berry of the Arctic. The pale orange berries resemble raspberries and grow on small plants at the edge of the wetlands. Cloudberries

Cloudberry

Labrador tea

are very soft, almost mushy, and have an unusual flavor. They taste a little like melons with crunchy seeds. In Norway they are sometimes stewed and eaten with milk and sugar.

After dinner, I often gathered a few sprigs of Labrador tea and steeped them in a cup of hot water. It makes a slightly piney, refreshing drink. Labrador tea has been used as a tea substitute in the North for hundreds of years.

The number of different plants that grow on the tundra is not very great when compared to warmer climates, but each one contributes to the cycle of life in the Arctic. Some become food for animals. Lichens slowly break down rocks into dirt. Eventually, every plant dies and decomposes, enriching the thin tundra soil. Decomposition takes a long time in the Arctic, for bacteria work very slowly in the cold.

As a traveler on the tundra, one quickly learns to recognize most of the plants, for they appear over and over again. Their small, simple beauty is there, each summer, adding color to the land.

Chapter 4

Birds and Bugs

A BIG, white bird glided silently over the snow-covered tundra. Then it flared its wings and landed softly on a knoll. After fluffing its feathers, the snowy owl searched the land with its large yellow eyes. The spring sun had begun to melt hollows around each rock, and a few brown blades of grass were showing through the snow. For the old owl it had been a good winter. Lemmings were plentiful and the bird had eaten well. Now the days were getting longer and soon the nesting season would begin again. Already the ptarmigan were proclaiming their nesting territories. The male ptarmigan perched on rocks and cackled loudly, warning other males to stay away. Near the river, ravens soared along the cliffs, searching for good nesting sites among the ledges.

The snowy owl, ptarmigan, and raven live on the tundra all year long. They have learned to survive the cold and darkness of the Arctic winter and will not leave the North unless food becomes desperately scarce. For about eight months each year they are the only birds commonly found in the northern lands.

With the coming of spring, however, other birds migrate to the tundra. Many make long and difficult flights. These are the summer residents, and they come north each year to raise their young in the Arctic.

Waterfowl, like geese and ducks, arrive by the millions to nest in the marshes. Gulls and other shore birds take over the gravel beaches, while smaller birds, such as the Lapland longspur, find nesting spots on the tundra hills. A few falcons and eagles also come north to nest in cliffs. Large or small, all of the birds have one thing in common, they all nest on the ground. Tree-nesting birds do not migrate to the tundra.

Many of the birds arrive in May, before the thaw has cleared the land. They must scratch about in the snow to find seeds and the remains of last year's plants until new growth emerges and insects hatch. The birds come north early, despite the poor food and frequent storms, to establish their territories. These early birds may not get the worm, but they do get first choice of nesting sites. (Later birds don't get any worms either, since there are no worms in the Arctic.) By early June the weather has usually improved enough so that nesting may begin.

Snowy owls nest along the Arctic coast where the

lemming population is the highest, for lemmings are their chief food. During the courtship, a male owl will catch a lemming and offer it to a female. If she accepts, they become a pair for the season and raise a brood. The female selects a dry spot on the tundra and prepares the nest. Usually it is just a shallow hole scraped out of the ground. When the female lays her first egg in the hole she begins sitting on the egg immediately. Other eggs follow as the month progresses.

After the eggs hatch, the male owl provides most of the food for the family. Since there is no darkness that time of year, he hunts by daylight. Stationed on a high point near the nest, the male watches for movement on the tundra. If he spots a lemming in the grass, the owl will swoop down and attack with sharp talons. If the owl is

successful, the lemming is carried back to the nest where the female tears it into bite-sized pieces to feed the young.

It requires a lot of pieces of lemming to raise a little snowy owl. Each owlet will eat about one hundred and fifty lemmings from the time it hatches until it is able to hunt on its own. Some summers lemmings are everywhere, but in other years they are scarce.

Snowy owls adjust the size of their brood to the lemming population. When lemmings are plentiful, an owl may lay eight or nine eggs. In another year, the same owl might lay only three. If lemmings are very scarce, snowy owls may not nest at all. That winter, if the owls cannot find food, they will leave the tundra, sometimes flying as far south as the United States.

Ptarmigan can usually find plenty of food in all seasons, for their diet is mostly plants. These chickenlike birds eat leaves and berries in the summer and the buds of dwarf willow after the snows come. Ptarmigan even use the snow to help them stay warm in winter. During blizzards they may bury themselves in drifts and remain covered until the storm is over.

We had been in the barren lands for six days before we came across a group of ptarmigan. Late one afternoon we pulled our canoes out on a rocky shore, and as we started lugging packs up the steep bank, a funny, cackling laughter rang out. It was an almost-human sound. The noise was coming from a thicket of dwarf spruce at the top of the bank. Next to the spruce was a flat area, ideal for camping.

I could not see the birds, but they continued to scold us as we spread our tents on the lichen-covered ground. The ptarmigan had probably never seen humans before, but they knew these two-legged creatures were invading their territory. As we finished staking down the tents, a swarm of hungry mosquitoes descended. I pulled on my headnet, found my binoculars, and went off to look for the birds.

Ptarmigan are masters of camouflage. In winter they are completely white except for a bit of black on their tail. As the snow melts, the white feathers are shed, and

mottled brown ones grow in their place. This coloring blends in well with the summer tundra.

The birds would have been very hard to find if they had stayed still and kept their beaks shut. As it was, the ptarmigan kept on cackling as I pushed my way through the brush, giving themselves away. They occasionally took short flights and landed in the thick growth, lost from view. But in a while a head would pop up and a bird would begin strutting around and making noise. They seemed to be as curious about me as I was about them. Later, the birds quieted down, allowing us to eat and sleep in peace.

Waterfowl are among the most common birds on the tundra in summer. We often came upon small flocks of Canada geese as we paddled down the rivers, as well as many families of ducks, usually mergansers. Occasionally, as we rounded a bend, three or four swans would be feeding in the shallows. All of these birds had flown a long way to get here. The swans had probably wintered on the east or west coast of the United States while the ducks and geese may have traveled from the Gulf of Mexico.

Of all the birds that migrate to the tundra, the Arctic terns make one of the longest flights. These slim, white birds begin their travels near Antarctica and, flying far out at sea, return to the Arctic tundra to nest each year. The distance they fly is nearly equal to a trip around the world. To the Eskimos they are the "bird of light" for they signal the return of the long days.

Arctic terns nest on gravel beaches that often run along the bank of a tundra river. The terns like their privacy and become very annoyed when canoes enter their territory. Frequently, as we paddled down a fast-moving river, we were attacked by these spirited birds.

The terns would fly overhead, chattering at us from above, and then dive, aiming for the back of someone's head. Barely missing, they would soar upward and prepare for another attack. They seemed to enjoy this sport,

for they would follow our canoes long after we had passed their nest.

Watching Arctic terns maneuver, one begins to see how they can migrate so far every year. They are very streamlined birds, and their long, pointed wings have the steady beat of an Olympic rowing crew. Each stroke sends them forward with effortless grace. They can also hover in the air, and then drop, beak first, to the river and come up with a minnow. Even after many Arctic tern attacks, I never tired of watching them fly.

Most of the birds lay their eggs in early June. The geese build grass nests in the marshes and line them with down plucked from their breasts. The female lays one egg each day, but does not sit on them until all of her eggs, usually three to eight, have been laid. In the meantime, she keeps the eggs hidden with a layer of grass over the nest. Arctic fox are fond of goose eggs and a gull or a jaeger will also steal eggs from another bird.

The eggs do not begin to develop until the female sits on them. For about three weeks she keeps them warm through snow storms, rain and sleet, until they all hatch on the same day.

Loons nest in the wetlands too, but they must find sites right next to the water. These big northern birds are built for swimming and diving and spend most of their life in the water. Their legs are placed so far back on their body, they can hardly walk on land. They are excellent divers and live on fish they catch far below the surface. Loons are easy to recognize by their beautiful black and white markings and their unusual calls. They make a variety of sounds, some of which are like hysterical laughter or "as crazy as a loon." A low, whistling loon call drifting over a tundra lake on a still evening somehow makes the silence of the wilderness seem even deeper.

Most birds hatch in late June when food on the tundra becomes plentiful. Plants are sending out tender green shoots and the waters are full of fish. And about this time each year an incredible number of insects emerge.

There are more mosquitoes in, on, and over the tundra than anywhere else in the world. The cold Arctic seems a strange place for bugs, but the endless swamps and ponds created by permafrost become giant mosquito breeders when warmed by the midnight sun. From Siberia to Alaska and all across the barren lands, little wriggling mosquito larvae emerge from the water to form clouds of flying, biting bugs.

As they hatch, billions are eaten by birds and fish, but there are more than enough mosquitoes to go around. Mosquitoes are an important part of the tundra food chain and are one of the few living things in the Arctic that seem to welcome the presence of humans.

The best defense against the hoards of bugs is heavy clothing. We wore tough, bite-proof khaki shirts and pants. As our guide suggested, we sealed the fronts of our shirts and the cuffs with Velcro. This kept the bugs, which were thicker than polka dots, from crawling between the buttons. A headnet is essential to keep them away from your face. Insect repellent helps, but it is no substitute for good clothing.

We usually did not have problems with bugs while canoeing on the river, but in the evening, if the wind let up, mosquitoes appeared in droves. Dinner was eaten standing up, facing the breeze, headnet slightly raised. When sketching, I wore thin leather gloves and learned to keep my pants tucked in my boots. Going to the bathroom in the open with clouds of bugs ready and waiting was always an exciting experience. A fresh coating of insect repellent below the waist helped a lot.

Even when it was windy, bugs were always thick in the shelter of a ravine or bush. The first rule of the summer tundra is: Never go anywhere without taking a headnet.

Blackflies were sometimes worse than mosquitoes. Blackflies are little flies that breed in running water and give a nasty, swelling bite. They are especially good at creeping under headnets and don't seem to mind the wind. They just cling to your clothing on the downwind side. On warmer nights, I sometimes awoke to a pattering on the walls of the tent. It sounded like rain, but it was blackflies, trying to find a way inside.

Swimming proved to be the best remedy for bug bites. The cool water had a soothing effect on the swelling and itching. It was not easy, however, to get in or out of the water without being bitten all over. I tried many different approaches. Lots of swatting and hopping around worked best.

Not all of the tundra insects are bloodthirsty. There are several other kinds of flies, as well as butterflies, moths, and bumblebees. They are even found in the high Arctic. Up there, the bumblebees are fatter and hairier than those of the southern tundra. This helps them handle the cold. In contrast, the butterflies throughout the tundra are quite small. When they are not flying, the butterflies spread their wings to the sun, collecting solar heat for their tiny bodies. Like bees and butterflies anywhere, they gather pollen and nectar from the tundra flowers. The flowers, in turn, are pollinated by the insects as they fly from blossom to blossom.

Most of the birds that migrate to the tundra feast on insects and plants, but some are hunters of larger game. The falcons, hawks, owls, and eagles that nest in the Arctic hunt small animals to feed themselves and their young. All these birds have excellent vision and little escapes their sight in the treeless, open country.

The peregrine falcon and gyrfalcon are the swiftest flyers. Their long, pointed wings and slender tails are made for speed and maneuverability. The falcons use their flying skill to hunt birds in midair. Birds make up most of their diet.

Peregrine falcons have become very rare. Once peregrines nested throughout North America, but in the late 1940s their numbers began to decline. Now they are common only in the Far North.

The decline of peregrines was eventually linked to DDT, a pesticide once widely used. Pesticides are designed to kill insects, not birds, but when they were first employed, little was known about their long-reaching effects. Small birds ate insects contaminated with DDT, and the peregrines ate the small birds. This left high levels of pesticide in the peregrines' bodies, which affected the formation of eggshells. Peregrine eggshells became so thin that they broke in the nest. Fewer peregrines hatched with each passing year.

DDT was not used on the tundra. The peregrines and

their prey became contaminated when they migrated to the farmlands of the United States. The peregrines that nested in the United States were almost completely destroyed. In the Arctic, more birds survived.

DDT is no longer used in the United States and there are programs underway to restore the peregrine falcon. Young birds and eggs are taken from the Arctic, raised by hand, and then released in areas where peregrines once nested. Slowly the falcons are returning, but DDT is still used in other places in the world. Such chemicals threaten life, no matter where they enter the food chain.

While canoeing in the barren lands, we got a close look at a pair of nesting peregrines. We had put ashore just ahead of a long stretch of rapids and were climbing a big hill that ended in cliffs overlooking the river. From there we could study the rapids and plan a route through.

As we neared the top of the hill, two peregrines came hurtling out of the sky, crying *kree...kree...kree,* and diving with their wings held close to their bodies. These were the same dives peregrines use in hunting, which can reach 300 kilometers per hour (186 miles per hour). People dropped to the ground as the birds swooped down on them, but the peregrines never touched anyone; they just came very close.

With binoculars I could see why they were upset. On

a little ledge near the top of the cliff were three white balls of fluff. Except for their beaks, they did not look much like birds. But in less than a month, these downy blobs would be flying almost as well as their parents.

Gyrfalcons are strictly birds of the Far North. They occur all around the Arctic, as do peregrines, but they do not migrate much further south than the taiga. Although they have not been exposed to as many pesticides, they are still threatened by humans.

Gyrfalcons are found in different color phases at different locations in the Arctic. The colors range from black to gray to almost pure white. The big white birds

have been prized as hunting falcons since the Middle Ages. They were kept by royalty in Europe, but were especially valued by sheiks and kings of the Middle East. With the recent petroleum boom in the Middle East, gyrfalcons are once again in demand as status symbols. A pure white bird may be worth over forty thousand dollars. This has lead to illegal trapping and smuggling of gyrfalcons.

Ravens look like crows, but are much larger. They are the only birds that live on the tundra year around as well as south of the treeline. They are found from the Arctic to Mexico. These intelligent birds can survive almost anywhere because they will eat almost anything. Ravens eat both plants and animals, but much of their food is carrion, animals that are already dead.

Ravens are great scavengers and soar high above the tundra looking for the carcass of a caribou or a ground squirrel or perhaps a wolf. They are very good at cleaning up the scraps from another animal's kill. I occasionally saw ravens on the barren lands, but they are easier to find in Arctic villages. There, they wait on build-ings and power poles to see what tidbits are thrown out in the garbage.

SOMETIME IN AUGUST, when the crowberries ripen to a rich crow black, the migrant birds begin to grow restless on the tundra. Summer is ending, and with it go the insects and fresh green shoots. In flocks the birds begin to leave the northern lands. Soon just a few feathers remain on the nesting grounds. Once again the snowy owl, ptarmigan, and raven have the tundra skies to themselves.

Chapter 5

Small Animals in the Cold

WHEN the ground squirrel came out of its burrow after the long winter it was thin and hungry. Nearly half its body weight had been used up during the eight months of hibernation. "*Sik-sik*," it called, as it ran across the snow and down into a small ravine. At the bottom of the ravine, willow twigs were sticking up through the drifts. The ground squirrel nibbled at them hungrily. The wind was sharp and cold, but the sun warmed the ground squirrel's fur as it chewed a tender bud. The animal had lived through another winter and would soon begin looking for a mate.

Only a few small animals are capable of surviving the Arctic winters. The ground squirrels hibernate, but the other animals remain active. It is a critical season for them, for they must protect themselves from the intense cold and find food on the frozen tundra. The smallest animals, shrews, mice, lemmings, and weasels, spend the winter beneath the snow. These animals do not have long fur or large body mass and need extra protection from the cold. Below the snow they are sheltered from the wind, and temperatures are much warmer than in the frigid air above. Dry snow is full of trapped air and makes a good insulator despite the fact it is cold.

Larger animals, like the Arctic fox and Arctic hare, grow thick coats of fur. They live out on the snow all winter long, seeking shelter in a snowdrift only in the worst storms.

All of the animals on the tundra, except for fish and insects, are warm-blooded. There are no frogs, turtles, toads, or snakes in the tundra ponds and marshes. These cold-blooded animals can't live in the Arctic where the climate would keep them inactive most of the time. Only birds and mammals, animals that regulate their own body heat, can manage the tundra winters on land.

Ground squirrels are true hibernators. After they have raised their litters in the spring, the parents and the young ground squirrels spend the summer eating and putting on fat. Fat is very important to all animals in the Arctic. It is rich in calories and provides a layer of insulation from the cold. When the ground squirrel hibernates, stored fat will be its only source of food. As autumn approaches ground squirrels squabble over the best burrows, but eventually each one will find a place to spend the winter.

In true hibernation the body functions slow down dramatically, until the animal is barely alive. The ground squirrel's heart slows from two hundred beats per minute to only five or ten. At the same time its breathing rate goes down and its temperature drops to just above freezing. True hibernation is quite different from a sleeping state. Bears pass the winter in a deep sleep, but their temperature remains near normal. The bear's other body functions slow down only slightly.

At some unknown signal the ground squirrel's hibernation ends. Heart rate and breathing speed up, bringing the animal's temperature back to normal. The ground squirrel awakens in the spring, and the cycle begins again.

Lemmings spend the winter eating and sleeping in tunnels under the snow. Lemmings, furry-footed animals about the size of a hamster, are the most abundant animals in some parts of the tundra. In the winter they eat dormant plants, living on the stored carbohydrates. Because they remain active, they are the prey that keep the snowy owl and fox alive through the dark months, as well as in the summer.

Lemmings are terrific breeders. Unlike most small animals in the Arctic, they do not wait for summer to begin reproducing. Instead, they have their first litter in March, beneath the snow. By the time the snow melts, a pair of lemmings may have had six or seven litters. Each litter consists of four to eight little lemmings. These new lemmings begin reproducing when they are twenty-five days old, making more lemmings. The original pair may be great-grandparents several times over when the thaw arrives. Of course, not all of these lemmings survive, but when conditions are right, lemmings reproduce in tremendous numbers.

Lemming colonies generally follow four-year cycles. In the first year of the cycle, lemmings are scarce. That summer the Arctic fox will have few kits, and the snowy owl may not nest. In the second year, lemmings increase a little, and their runways can be spotted occasionally in the grass. By the third year they are very numerous. Fox and owls raise larger families then, for it is easy to find food.

At the peak of the lemming cycle, they seem to be everywhere, squeaking, fighting, and scurrying about. All this activity attracts a host of predators. Hawks, gulls, jaegers, and ravens converge on the lemmings, as well as fox and owls. Even the big tundra wolves can find enough lemmings to satisfy their hunger. As the predators feast, the lemmings continue to reproduce. There may be so many lemmings that the area is stripped of vegetation.

In Scandinavia, when overcrowding becomes this serious, the brown lemmings begin to migrate. They start moving in irregular patterns, but all in one general direction. Soon thousands of lemmings are streaming over the tundra. When they come to a river, they plunge in and swim across. Some drown, some are eaten by fish, but most reach the other side. The migration continues until the lemmings reach the sea. They begin swimming again, but this time the lemmings all drown.

The drowning was once thought to be a mass suicide by crazed, overcrowded lemmings. More likely, it is just bad judgment on their part. Lemmings are small and have no way of estimating the size of the ocean. From the shore it probably appears to them as another large river.

Not all lemming communities undergo these mass migrations, but all experience population cycles. In other places, lemmings that are not eaten by predators starve to death when the food is exhausted. After the winter in a peak lemming year, only a few lemmings are left to begin the cycle again. The tundra plants that were chewed down by the lemmings are fertilized by the droppings and bodies of the dead animals. This nourishes the large root systems and the plants recover quickly.

At the end of the cycle, the foxes and owls that have become more numerous suddenly find themselves without enough food for the winter. The owls may leave the tundra. A fox will travel long distances trying to find new things to eat. But there is little on the tundra besides lemmings that can provide food for a large number of foxes. In the low-lemming winter, many foxes starve. In this way the fox population goes up and down with the lemming.

The Arctic fox is a beautiful creature. It moves with an easy trot across the tundra while its long, full tail streams out behind. Unlike its southern relatives, an Arctic fox has a very short muzzle and small ears. This helps reduce heat loss from its body and gives the adults a puppyish look.

The coat of the Arctic fox is especially luxurious. It is brown in summer and may look rather ratty as the foxes shed. When autumn approaches, however, the brown hair is replaced with a thick fur of pure white. The coat has two parts. The outer layer is made up of long, shiny guard hairs that shed rain and snow. Beneath that is a thick underfur. The underfur is soft and very fine. It is the fox's insulation against the cold.

Arctic foxes are solitary creatures and have no home except the open tundra. For most of the year they wander and hunt by themselves. Sometimes a fox will follow a polar bear out on the ice and live on scraps from the bear's kill, but generally they hunt small animals on land.

In the spring Arctic foxes stop wandering long enough to raise a family. They find mates and dig dens for their young. Often the same dens are used each season. When food is plentiful, the female fox, or vixen, may give birth to ten or twelve kits. The kits are born in early June. The family stays near the den until the young are old enough to hunt for themselves. By late July, the kits are nearly full grown. Then the foxes separate and begin their solitary ways. The den is used only when raising a family.

When winter comes howling across the tundra, an Arctic fox, like a wolf or husky dog, can sleep comfortably right on the snow. It curls up tightly and tucks its head underneath its tail. The thick coat of white fur keeps it warm and hidden.

Not all Arctic foxes become white in the winter. A few are silver-gray. These are called blue foxes because their coat has a faintly bluish tinge.

Both white and blue foxes have been trapped by people in the Arctic for centuries. The early Eskimos acquired their first guns and cooking pots by trading the skins of the Arctic fox. Trapping is still an important source of income for many people in the North. The furs are made into expensive coats that are sold in cities around the world.

In the Soviet Union trapping is big business. Trappers even put out feeding stations for the fox, especially in years when lemmings are scarce. This saves the fox from starvation, only to face the jaws of the steel trap.

Foxes are often thought of as sly, crafty animals that cause trouble. It is true they are intelligent, clever hunters, but their reputation as villains is undeserved. The Arctic fox, like its cousin the red fox, which sometimes hunts the tundra, lives on small rodents, berries, and scraps left by other animals. In this way, the fox helps maintain the balance of life in the tundra community.

Where animals are trapped or hunted, they become naturally shy of humans. There were blue foxes on the island where I lived in Alaska. No one bothered them there. The foxes were not tame, but they were curious and not afraid of people.

Another animal that has adapted to the climate in ways similar to the Arctic fox is the Arctic hare. In summer these big rabbits are dark-colored and blend in with the tundra. In winter, their coat changes to white. The Arctic hares also do not have a permanent home.

They roam the tundra, eating grass, willow twigs, and other plants.

We came across an Arctic hare on the barren lands while exploring a big esker. The top of the esker was sandy and set with black rocks, like the surface of the moon. Among the rocks was a dark gray hare.

Right away I could see this was no ordinary rabbit. Arctic hare are very big, well over a half meter tall when sitting. Instead of a plump, bunny-like body, this hare had muscles that bulged beneath its skin. The animal was cautious but not frightened by our presence. When someone approached to take a picture, it ran a short distance, then stopped. Its movement was not like other rabbits, for instead of hopping, Arctic hares run with a strong, loping gait. In the high Arctic, when these rabbits are alarmed, they have been known to stand upright and bound away like kangaroos.

"Our" hare was not alarmed, though, and eventually loped down the esker and out across the tundra. We watched it disappear in the distance under a bright, cloudless sky.

The next day a storm full of cold, driving rain kept us off the river. We rested safe and dry in our tents which flapped and billowed in the wind. But I wondered what the fox and hare did in such weather out on the tundra.

for wolves may be following the herd. Adult caribou have big round hooves that carry them easily through soft snow and muddy swamps. The young calves need better footing if they are to escape from predators.

The calves grow rapidly on the nourishing milk. After ten days of nursing and traveling, they have already doubled their birth weight. By late June, when they are a month old, the young caribou are almost weaned. The snow is nearly gone by then, and the herd has reached its summer range far up in the tundra. The bulls, which began migrating later, now join the cows and calves.

On the summer range, small groups of caribou

wander about the tundra munching grass and willow. This is a welcome change from their winter diet of dry lichen. Yet even now, the deer are seldom still. Caribou do not graze like cattle, standing placidly in the field. They are constantly moving, trotting into the wind, pausing now and then to grab a mouthful of food. This helps them avoid the swarms of bugs and flies that follow them. It serves another purpose as well. The tundra is not a lush pasture. The plants are small and grow slowly. A large herd of caribou could quickly destroy the vegetation if they stayed in one place for long, but because they keep moving, no area is overgrazed.

In the barren lands the caribou spread their range even further by making a midsummer migration. In July they go south almost to the treeline, and then turn around and head north again in August. They continue north until the snow comes. Then they turn once again and begin the long trek back to the forest.

Each herd has its own migration route and calving grounds. Some travel long distances, and some not so far. In Greenland and the high Arctic, where there are no forests, smaller herds migrate on the tundra all year. The largest herds, however, are on the mainland. They travel to the taiga each winter. In the shelter of the trees, the snow is softer than on the tundra, and the caribou can dig for lichens with their hooves.

Canoeing north in July, we hoped to intercept the Beverly herd coming south on their midsummer migration. The herds are named for their calving grounds and this herd calves near Beverly Lake.

Long before we saw any caribou, it was clear we were following a route the animals had used for many years. Caribou trails crisscrossed the tundra everywhere and old antlers lay about. Both male and female caribou grow antlers. Every year these are shed on the spring migration. A short walk on the tundra near our first campsites always produced at least one big antler. Sometimes the antlers were still attached to the skull, the remains of a wolf kill. As we traveled north, antlers became less common, but there were still many trails and the cracked bones of caribou littered the tundra. Bones decompose very slowly in the cold. Some bleached, white fragments may have been lying there for fifty or

sixty years. Others still had blood and hair on them.

There were other signs marking the caribou route. Ancient hunters had placed *inushuks*, piles of stones, at intervals along the top of some ridges. These stones were meant to resemble standing men. The hunters hoped the inushuks would frighten the caribou and direct the herd toward a river crossing where they lay waiting. Since these men had only spears and bows, their best chance at the caribou would come when the deer were swimming the river.

Near our campsites we found stone flakes, chipped from the spearheads these people had made while they waited for the caribou to appear. For these tribes, the caribou provided food, clothing, and hides to cover their tents. Not finding the herd could mean starvation for their people that winter.

We faced no such difficulties as we searched day by day for the caribou. We were simply growing anxious to see these wandering deer.

We had just finished lunch one day and were paddling easily, getting back into the rhythm of the river, when my canoe partner glanced to shore.

"There they are," he said.

We could not see the deer, but there was a small forest of antlers moving along the top of the bank. We ran our canoes aground and dashed up a small hill.

The caribou were right there. Bulls with big racks of antlers, cows, and calves trotted by, snorting and grunting. A sound like cracking sticks came from their feet as they passed. It was a small herd, about one hundred animals. They moved together in a tightly packed bunch, flowing around rocks and bushes. They seemed to have only one mind. The caribou crossed the flat land swiftly and disappeared behind a hill. It was all over in a few minutes. Only stragglers were left. They ran nervously back and forth, far out on the tundra, unsure of what to do.

There are about two hundred thousand caribou in the Beverly herd. Sometimes they migrate all at once, sometimes in small groups. Another herd almost charged through our camp the next day during breakfast.

We saw many more caribou during the rest of the trip, but the main herds slipped by unnoticed. Occasionally their barnyard smell was in the air, and once we saw tracks where thousands of deer had passed.

The caribou we saw were strong, healthy animals. They moved across the bumpy tundra with a prancing gait, heads held high. Big hooves and strong legs carried them through the meadows and up the hills with ease. A person on foot could not begin to match their pace.

Caribou are always on the move, but occasionally we found them napping on the wide sand beaches along the river. There, they could lie down and rest in safety. Wolves were about, but they could not approach the caribou across the sand without being seen. If the caribou were attacked, they would swim the river, for they are excellent swimmers. On the beach the bulls laid their heads to one side and rested their antlers in the sand. It must have been a big relief, for the racks are very heavy.

In summer, while the antlers are growing, they are covered with a velvet skin. As winter approaches, the caribou scrape off the velvet, leaving the hard bone underneath. The antlers are impressive, but they are not effective weapons. The caribou rely on speed and stamina to stay away from their chief predator, the tundra wolf.

Tundra wolves are the largest of all wolves. The males may weigh over 45 kilograms (99 pounds) and females slightly less. Some are black or gray, but many are almost white. Tundra wolves have pale eyes, excellent hearing and vision, and a very sensitive nose. They can sprint with great speed and trot for hours without stopping. Their jaws can crush the largest bone in a caribou's body.

Once there were wolves almost everywhere in the northern part of the world. They lived in the mountains, deserts, plains, and forests of the United States and Canada and throughout Europe and Asia. Today most of those wolves are gone. They are still fairly common, however, in the tundra and forests of Alaska and Canada.

Wolves are creatures of the wild. Wherever the wilderness is cleared to make way for farms and fields, wolves are hunted and trapped. Early ranchers and herdsmen thought of wolves only as dangerous animals that killed livestock. They believed wolves were also a threat to their families, and so the wolf came to be feared by almost everyone.

Biologists have only recently begun studying wolves. As these studies progress, we are learning, as the Eskimos and Indians always knew, that wolves are not dangerous to people. Unfortunately, they have been misrepresented for centuries.

Tundra wolves are social animals that live and hunt in family groups, or packs. For most of the year they follow the migrating caribou. Hunting the caribou is life itself to the tundra wolf. But everything in nature is balanced. The caribou feeds the wolf, but the wolf also helps the caribou.

How can killing caribou help them? The answer lies in which caribou the wolves kill. Hunting is hard, dangerous work for wolves. Healthy caribou are fast and difficult to catch. Their hooves can cripple a wolf or break its jaw, and a badly injured wolf is as good as dead. Wolves understand this and seldom hunt healthy adults. Instead, they concentrate on calves, old caribou, and sick or lame animals.

Wolves may test a small band of caribou by chasing them. If the caribou are strong, the wolves quickly lose interest. But if one of the animals is slow or weak, the wolves will single it out and keep up the chase. If the caribou tires, a swift wolf will bring it down by clamping its jaws on the animal's neck. The lighter and faster female wolves often make the kill.

By hunting the weakest animals, the wolves help keep the herd strong. Only the best caribou, those that escape the wolves, are left to breed.

Only about one chase in fourteen actually ends in a kill, but then the whole pack shares in the meat. Wolves do not eat in a wild frenzy, but have good communal manners. They eat as much as they can hold, though, for they may go without food for many days.

Tundra wolves are timid and curious about humans. Our guide, Alex, told us of wolves that had wandered into his camp, looking around, and then wandered off again. Several times he had caught small wolf pups near a den. He photographed them and then put them back, while the adult wolves watched from a distance. Very few wild animals will allow people anywhere near their young.

Around Arctic settlements, where wolves are common, they do not bother people; only a wolf that is sick with rabies is feared. Sled dogs are actually more dangerous. Almost every year in the North, a child is killed by a dog that has broken loose.

I was sitting outside my tent one morning, when a wolf came over the hill headed in my direction. It was pale gray and looked like a big dog as it trotted through a fellfield. I whistled softly to the people in camp. The wolf also heard and immediately changed course to avoid us. As it walked along the side of the hill, I whistled again, this time loudly. The wolf stopped, looked at me over its shoulder, and then went off. I guess we were both on our way to breakfast.

After breakfast, oatmeal and tea, as usual, we packed our tents and set off down the river once more. We had only gone a short way before wolves started howling. A long, melodious *OWOOOOOOOOOoooooooooo* echoed from the hills and riverbanks. The sound changed pitch as it went on and then faded away, only to begin again. Hearing wolves can be more mysterious than seeing them.

We paddled to shore, pushing our canoes to a halt in the thick grass along the bank, and scrambled up one of the short, steep hills that overlooked the river. At the top of the hill was a clump of spruce trees with a series of holes leading beneath the roots. The holes were big enough for a person to crawl into. The howling stopped, and Alex peered into each hole. After checking them all, he silently motioned toward one entrance. I lay down at the mouth of the tunnel and leaned my head into the opening.

The den was very dark and smelled like urine. As my eyes adjusted, I could just make out the heads and paws of two large wolf pups. The pups scratched at the sand on the den floor but made no other sound. When one of them turned, the dim light caught its eye, and a yellow gleam shone out of the darkness. The adult wolves, which had done the howling, were somewhere close by, but they stayed out of sight.

Tundra wolves, like Arctic foxes, den only when they have young. For a time, the pack, usually five to eight adults, must stop following the caribou and stay near the den. Good denning sites are scarce on the tundra, and so the same ones are used again and again.

Only the dominant female in the pack breeds and has pups. She nurses her pups while they are small, but they soon begin eating meat. The other wolves in the pack help feed the pups by catching lemmings, or ground squirrels, or birds, whatever can be found in the wolves' territory. The meat is swallowed and carried back to the den in the wolf's stomach. When the pups nuzzle the adult, the meat is regurgitated for them to eat. When they are not hunting, adults take turns watching the little wolves. Sometimes wolves spend hours just playing.

If no big game is near the den, it can be a hungry time for the wolves. It takes a lot of small animals to feed a pack.

Outside the den on the hill were fresh bones from a

calf caribou. The wolves must have caught this caribou during the midsummer migration.

By late summer the young wolves are big enough to join the hunt. Then the pack will leave the den area and begin following the caribou. As the caribou migrate back to the forest, the wolves will go with the herd.

The caribou on the fall migration look different from those that came north in the spring. Their coats are thick and the animals have put on weight. Even the calves have sprouted antlers.

During the winter the caribou wander the taiga. They rest on frozen lakes in the day, and then go into the forests to eat. Wolves hunt them among the trees.

Life is not easy for either the caribou or the wolf. In the first year about half of the calves and pups will die. Only the strongest young animals survive to make the trip back to the tundra in the spring.

In Alaska and Canada, wolves and caribou have roamed free on the tundra for thousands of years. Before they were hunted with guns, the herds were tremendous in size. Early explorers described their numbers in acres of animals. There were about three or four million caribou living in North America around 1900. Everyone thought such herds could never be threatened. Yet by 1950, in Canada, only two or three hundred thousand caribou remained.

Wolves were blamed for the decrease, and thousands of wolves were poisoned, trapped, or shot. But the wolves, which had always lived with the caribou, were not responsible for the decline. People were at fault. Guns made caribou easy to kill, and thousands of animals were slaughtered each year above and below the tree-line. Other caribou starved when forest fires destroyed the lichens in their winter feeding grounds.

When the real reasons for the decline of the caribou were recognized, the campaign to kill wolves was stopped and caribou hunting was regulated. The herds are increasing again, and the wolves are recovering too. But wolves are still feared and hunted by some people.

As for the caribou, they are like the buffalo that once roamed the western plains. Their fate is in the hands of men. They are free to wander the tundra as long as no one wants their land.

On the other side of the world, the story of the car-ibou has been very different. In Scandinavia and Siberia, the tundra is the home of the reindeer, a close relative of the North American caribou. Reindeer have been kept as domestic animals by Laplanders and the native people of Asia for centuries. Somehow these people were able to tame the wild deer enough to herd them like cattle. The reindeer make annual migrations just like the car-ibou, and the herdsmen follow their deer onto the tundra each year. The animals are kept for their milk, meat, and

hides. Some of the larger deer have been trained to pull sleds. In Siberia they have been ridden with saddles placed high on their shoulders.

Today reindeer herding is a large industry in Lapland and the Soviet Union. There are about a million domestic reindeer in Scandinavia and perhaps three times as many in Siberia. There are also wild herds. In a later chapter we learn more about the people who herd the deer.

Wolves are no friends to the reindeer herder. Every calf lost to a wolf means less money earned. As a result, the wolf has been hunted to extinction in Lapland. There are no reports on the fate of the wolves in Siberia.

Chapter 7

Muskoxen
and Bears

THOUSANDS of years ago, during the last ice age, woolly mammoths, saber-toothed cats, and muskoxen lived on the tundra. Stone-age men and wolves hunted these animals, in addition to caribou, following them across Siberia and into Alaska. At that time Alaska and Siberia were joined by a land bridge. The woolly mammoth and saber-toothed cat became extinct as the ice retreated. They may have been hunted out of existence or, perhaps, died out for other reasons. Their skeletons have been found buried in the tundra, along with whole mammoths, frozen and preserved in the permafrost. Today, the remains of the woolly mammoth and saber-toothed cat can only be seen in museums. The muskox, however, is still walking around on the tundra, nipping off shoots of dwarf willow. It is a living relic of the ice age.

Muskoxen resemble bison, but they are smaller and have very long coats. Both male and female muskoxen have large heads capped with sturdy, curving horns. The solid, powerful build of the animals make them appear larger than they actually are. The hump of a male musk-ox's shoulder is about as high as a man's chest. Females are slightly smaller. In spite of their name, muskoxen are not musky or related to oxen. They are a family of their own, distantly related to goats.

Muskoxen are true creatures of the tundra. They live only in the Arctic, surviving in some of the coldest, most desolate regions. They make no dens or shelters and spend all of their lives in the open. They never leave the tundra, although they do migrate short distances between their summer and winter ranges.

Muskoxen eat only plants. In summer, when the blue sky of the north is streaked with thin clouds, muskoxen graze slowly on tender grass and willow shoots that grow in moist areas. When winter comes, these areas are covered with a hard layer of snow. The muskoxen cannot dig through this layer, and so the herds move to higher, windswept ground to find food.

Imagine what it is like to be a muskox in winter. Many of these shaggy animals live on islands far up in the

Arctic Ocean where the winter darkness lasts for three or four months. The temperature rarely rises above –30° C (–22° F) and the wind makes it feel even colder. It is so cold that a person's fingers, unprotected by mittens, would be frostbitten in seconds. The rolling land is completely covered with snow except for the windy hilltops. There the muskoxen gather to search for a bit of crowberry or bilberry to eat. If a crust of snow forms on the hill, a muskox will paw it, or drop its head and crash through the crust with its nose. All this for a few bites of frozen food. Yet the muskox is accustomed to the cold and darkness. As long as food is available, they amble about the hills in apparent comfort.

The secret of their winter survival is a superior, two-layered coat. The outer layer of hair is black or dark brown and very long. It hangs down to the muskox's white ankles and sways, as the animal moves, like a

grass skirt. Beneath this guard hair is a thick underwool called *qiviut*. Qiviut is much finer and softer than sheep's wool and gives good protection against the wind and cold.

Muskoxen were plentiful in the Arctic before whaling ships came to the North. The animals lived in many regions throughout the tundra, and their only serious predator was the wolf. However, when guns were introduced by whalers and trappers, hunting increased until the muskox was close to extinction.

The defensive behavior of muskoxen made them especially easy to kill. Muskoxen live in herds that average about fifteen animals. When a muskox herd senses danger, they do not run away or attack. Instead, the adults form a tight circle around the young. The big animals face outward and defend the circle with their sharp horns.

This is a good defense against wolves. As long as the muskoxen stand fast, the wolves have little chance of making a kill.

Early Eskimos also hunted muskoxen, using bows made from muskox horn and stone-tipped arrows. They, too, found the circle difficult to penetrate.

The circle defense, however, was useless against men with guns. Hunters easily killed whole herds of muskoxen. The animals just stood there, trying to maintain their circle, while they were shot down, one by one.

The crews of whaling ships killed many herds this way for fresh meat. After natives acquired guns, they also began killing more muskoxen for food. If this wasn't enough, muskox hides became popular in Europe as carriage robes. Thousands of animals were slaughtered just for their skins. In Alaska, the muskox was completely destroyed. By 1900, only a few, remote herds were left. After living through the ice age, the muskox was about to go the way of the woolly mammoth.

Finally, in 1917, Canada passed laws to protect the remaining animals. Slowly, the herds began to increase. When the herds became large enough, some animals were captured and taken back to Alaska and other places where they had lived. There are now over fifty thousand muskoxen in North America. Limited hunting is once again allowed.

Most of the new herds are wild, but in Unalakeet, Alaska, about one hundred and fifty muskoxen are kept in a semidomestic herd. These animals have been raised by hand and are accustomed to people. Each spring, when the muskoxen shed their qiviut, a herder combs out the wool and collects it. In the wild the qiviut just falls out and blows across the tundra. The collected qiviut is spun into yarn, then knitted into expensive hats and scarves that are softer than cashmere, lightweight, and very warm. During the summer the muskoxen grow a new layer of qiviut for the winter to come.

I went looking for muskoxen with two friends as we neared the end of our trip. We had come far enough north to be in muskox territory, but had seen no animals along the river. A few tufts of qiviut had been found on bushes though. The bearded one, or *Oomingmak,* as Eskimos call the muskox, was out there somewhere.

We climbed a long sloping hill, hoping, but not really expecting, to see a muskox. Life on the tundra is thinly distributed because of the limited food supply. Chances of finding any animal in a few hours of walking are not good.

Reaching the top of the hill we scanned the surrounding country. The land below was folded and puckered in gentle ridges. Lakes shimmered in the afternoon light. On the far side of a pond, a kilometer away, a brown

lump stood motionless against the tundra. I carefully focused my binoculars and found, by amazing luck we had come upon a muskox. There were no other animals about, so this was probably a lone bull, which had left the herd.

Keeping low, we made our way down the exposed hillside. The muskox ambled off. I could not tell whether he sensed our presence or not. We went around a small lake and across a swamp. The muskox moved slowly uphill alowing us to get quite close. We could see the dark eyes in the great fuzzy head and the tan curl of the horns. The animal also saw us and began walking faster.

He disappeared into a clump of spruce downhill. When I saw him again, a few minutes later, he was just a speck, running hard across a distant meadow, in the autumn light.

This muskox was in the Thelon Game Sanctuary, near the center of the barren lands. Here, far from the sea, the herds were not slaughtered and continued to thrive. The sanctuary is a huge area where hunting is not permitted, but there are no fences or signs to separate it from the rest of the tundra. Although it is far north of the treeline, stands of big spruce grow close to the river. Beyond the trees it is open tundra again.

The mixture of trees and tundra attracts unexpected animals. A robin sang. That robin had flown over many kilometers of bare tundra to nest in a tree here near the river.

Moose were common here, too. Moose are normally forest animals, but they will live anywhere on the tundra if there is enough willow and alder to eat. The area is also home to one of the rarest tundra animals, the barren ground grizzly bear.

Only about a thousand barren ground grizzlies exist in North America. They live on the mainland tundra of Alaska and Canada, usually close to one of the rivers that flow to the polar sea. Barren ground grizzlies are big bears. They are similar to other grizzlies, except their fur is blond, almost as light as a polar bear.

Hiking on the tundra, I kept a wary eye out for these bears. Grizzly bears do not often bother people, but with bears one can never be sure. Occasionally, there were fresh tracks in the damp sand of a tundra circle. The print of a barren ground grizzly's paw is as big as a dinner plate, with deep impressions left by the long, curved claws. Each time I found tracks, I stopped and looked all around. Visibility is good on the tundra, but a bear could be hidden by any small hill or ravine.

In camp a bear alarm was tied to the canvas garbage bag each night. The alarm was a battery-powered buzzer

that would go off if the garbage was knocked over. The alarm never sounded. On this trip we neither saw nor heard a bear.

The natives call barren ground grizzlies "the blind bears," for their eyesight is very poor. They are not actually blind, but they use their nose to find most of their food.

These grizzlies eat almost anything they find on the tundra. Plants make up much of their diet. They graze in the meadows in summer and fatten up on dark blue bearberries in the fall. Bears must eat a lot of berries to satisfy even part of their needs.

The long claws and powerful shoulder muscles of grizzly bears are designed for digging up roots, but sometimes a bear will try to dig out a ground squirrel, lemming, or a wolf pup for a bit of meat.

These grizzlies eat meat whenever they can find it. Usually the meat is carrion, animals that are already dead. Grizzlies are great scavengers and can smell a caribou carcass a long way off. Bears prefer scavenging to hunting live game, but they are capable of killing muskoxen or caribou when they have the chance. Although bears walk with a heavy gait and appear rather clumsy and slow, when hunting or in danger, they can move very quickly. They are still not fast enough to chase a healthy caribou, though, and so will prey on weak or wounded animals.

When the snow returns to the tundra and covers the last of the berries, barren ground grizzlies look for a place to spend the winter. This might be a den in a hillside or just a cave dug in a deep snowdrift. There, protected from the worst of the cold, they sleep for several months, living on the fat of their bodies. This is a very deep sleep, but not the true hibernation of the ground squirrel. Bears may even awaken once or twice during the winter and take a walk on the snow before returning to their den.

During this sleep, sow bears give birth to twin cubs. The newborn cubs are very small and snuggle deep into their mother's fur to nurse and stay warm. While the winter wind blows across the tundra and the northern lights shine in the sky, the cubs eat and grow larger in the den beneath the snow.

In the spring the cubs will follow their mother as she roams the land. They stay with her for two or three years, sleeping together in a large den each winter. When they are able to take care of themselves, they will go off alone on the tundra.

Polar bears, the other bears of the Arctic, also have their cubs in snow caves on the tundra. Their dens are always near the ocean, for polar bears are not creatures of the land.

Polar bears are seal hunters. They spend most of their life on the ice floes of the Arctic Ocean hunting seal. Only sows that are having cubs make winter dens. Males and the other females continue to hunt all winter long. The Eskimos call them "the ever-wandering ones." Polar bears range over the entire Arctic Ocean and have been seen quite close to the North Pole.

In the summer, polar bears may come ashore, but they seldom go very far inland. On land they eat the same things that grizzlies eat, including the tundra berries. Since most Arctic villages are on the coast, people have more contact with polar bears than with barren ground grizzlies. Some polar bears may paw through garbage dumps near the villages. Because bears are hunters, they can be dangerous. They are not afraid of people and have been known to stalk and kill humans. Where polar bears are common, people usually carry guns if they are traveling on the tundra.

While polar bears *have* killed a few people, it is generally the other way around. Demand for polar bear hides led to increased killing of these animals by people until limits were established.

Muskoxen, barren ground grizzlies, polar bears, along with caribou and wolves are all animals that could have been hunted out of existence. Fortunately, the problems were recognized in time. While none of these animals are presently in danger from overhunting in North America, other difficulties, just as serious, exist.

These are all large, wild animals. They require lots of room and prefer to stay far away from human settlements. Not many people live on the tundra, so there is plenty of space for animals and humans alike. But the Arctic is fast becoming a new source for minerals, especially oil. This kind of exploration and development of wilderness areas always threatens the lives of animals that live there. If we wish to have animals in their natural state, we must make sure there is enough land set aside for them as well as for our own needs.

Chapter 8

People in the Arctic

WHEN explorers first went north, they were amazed by the hardy people they found living on the tundra. These people survived the coldest climate on earth in tents, igloos, and sod houses without the warmth of a wood fire. They hunted caribou and huge whales using only spears tipped with stone or bone. They endured long periods of darkness with just the light from a sputtering seal oil lamp.

If those same explorers went north today, they would see a different life in the Arctic: An Eskimo child riding a plastic tricycle down a dirt street lined with houses. Teams of geologists searching the tundra for mineral deposits. A young mother in Lapland buying milk and fresh vegetables at a store.

A dramatic change has come to the people, and this means changes for the land and animals as well.

For centuries the few people who lived in the North were isolated from the rest of the world. The climate and the roadless tundra were barriers that kept them cut off. They depended entirely upon their own skills for survival and the Arctic animals for food and clothing.

Some, like the Laplanders, herded reindeer, traveling to the tundra each summer. The Eskimos and others lived on the northern coasts where they hunted from the ocean as well as the land. The tundra, by itself, is a poor provider, and very few people lived on the inland tundra all year long.

All these people managed to live with the cold climate by making the most of what was available. They were clever inventors, giving us several things we use today. Skis were first devised by the Lapps to follow the reindeer. The Eskimos invented kayaks for hunting whale and seal. Parkas, not fires, kept the people of the Arctic warm.

Most of the early tundra dwellers wore a double suit of caribou skin clothing in the winter. The inner suit was sewn with the hair on the inside, towards the body. The outer suit had the hair on the outside, against the weather. These suits were loose and bulky, but actually not very heavy. Caribou hair is filled with air cells, and the hides were lightweight and good insulation. This clothing surpasses even modern materials for warmth and weight, but it is seldom made anymore.

The changes in Arctic life came slowly at first. Trappers, hunters, and whalers, introduced guns and iron tools, but the old ways of living from the land went on. Unlike the American West, no pioneer families went north to homestead. No one built railroads across the tundra.

The big changes began in the 1950s, when the airplane opened up the Arctic. Remote villages and camps could be reached in a few hours by air instead of months overland. Governments built houses and schools. Snowmobiles quickly took over from dog sleds. Military radar stations were set up. As the tundra became more accessible, the exploration for minerals began.

All this activity brought new people north. In Europe and Asia, mining operations now employ so many people that natives have become the minority. In North America the development is just beginning.

Lapland, in Northern Scandinavia, contains the smallest and most settled area of tundra in the world. This is the summer range for the Lapp reindeer herds. The reindeer are raised by Lapp families, who travel with the herds on their annual migrations.

In the past, the Lapp people (who call themselves

Saami) followed the deer on skis and sleds. It was a simple life, and the animals provided most of the food the family ate.

Today, herding is done with snowmobiles and motorcycles. The machines make the work easier, but it is still a cold and difficult job. Reindeer are now raised as a cash crop like cattle. Each year, part of the herd is sold to a slaughter house where the animals are butchered and packaged like beef. The Lapps still butcher a few deer for themselves, but most of the family's food is bought.

Less than ten percent of the Saami now herd reindeer. The rest work at regular jobs along with other Scandinavians who have moved north.

Although fewer Saami keep reindeer, the size of the individual herds has increased. Limits now regulate the total number of deer to prevent overgrazing the tundra.

The tundra is still open country in Lapland, but civilization is moving in. Villages are linked by paved roads. Power dams furnish electricity. New national parks encourage tourists and campers to visit the area. Each development means less tundra for reindeer and more people in the land of the midnight sun.

Building and development in Lapland is easier than in the rest of the tundra because there is no permafrost there. The warm ocean currents of the Gulf Stream keep Lapland a little milder than most of the Arctic.

Farther east, in Siberia, the tundra extends almost a third of the way around the Arctic Ocean. It is a thinly settled land with no network of roads, where winters are bitterly cold. The native people of the region, the Nenets, Evenk, Yakut, and Chukchi are the ancestors of the American Indian and Eskimo. Traditionally they were reindeer herders as well as hunters and trappers.

Today, some of these people operate the collective reindeer farms that have been organized by the Soviet Union. The herds produce tremendous quantities of meat, which is sold in Siberia and Japan. Reindeer herding is an efficient use of the tundra, for the deer require nothing except the plants that grow wild.

In summer, after school is out, the children of the herding people join their families on the tundra. They all live in big round tents, called *yarangas*, just as their

grandfathers did. Mail and supplies, however, may be delivered by helicopter, as they follow the deer.

There is special emphasis in the Soviet Union on developing the resources of the Arctic. Although most of the land remains wild, a city of two hundred and fifty thousand people has been built on the tundra at Norilsk. Norilsk is just north of the treeline near large deposits of copper, nickel, coal, and natural gas.

Most Arctic towns are overgrown villages, but Norilsk is a modern city. People live in apartment buildings and work in stores, factories, and offices. Children attend schools with indoor garden rooms full of plants and birds to brighten the Arctic winter.

Construction of large buildings or roads on the tundra requires special attention to the problems of permafrost. All buildings begin with an underground foundation. Where there is no permafrost, the foundation rests on rock or firm soil, which supports the weight of the building. Putting a foundation on permafrost, however, is like resting a building on frozen mud. As long as the permafrost remains frozen, it will give good support, but if the foundation warms, and thaws the permafrost, the building will sink into the ground or tip to one side.

To avoid these problems, structures are built on pilings that are set deep in the ground and kept very cold. Some buildings have an air space between the ground and the first floor to keep the pilings chilled. Others use pilings with built-in refrigeration systems.

If a road is needed on the tundra, it must be carefully constructed to avoid melting the permafrost. Most vehicles cannot be driven on the tundra in summer without causing serious damage. Ruts left by a truck or bulldozer allow the sun to melt the permafrost below the active layer. This leads to erosion that widens the ruts and further melts the permafrost with each passing summer. Eventually a gully can be formed.

Driving a truck only once over the tundra ground has resulted in gullies that could swallow the truck a few years later.

Tundra roads must be built on thick gravel pads to insulate them from the soil. This prevents the heat and weight of cars and trucks from thawing the permafrost. Improperly built roads soon become a boggy mess.

In Siberia, the many rivers are used for transportation. In the summer, boats and hydrofoils bring supplies inland from ports on the Arctic Ocean. During the winter, the frozen rivers become highways for truck traffic.

Alaska, across the Bering Straits from Siberia, is the site of another major development in the Arctic. In the

late 1960s, the largest oil field in North America was discovered on the tundra of the North Slope near Prudhoe Bay. This has brought sudden changes for the Eskimos of the area, the animals, and the land.

A pipeline was built from Prudhoe Bay across the entire state to bring the oil to an ice-free port. This pipeline was one of the largest, most expensive construction projects ever undertaken. About a third of the pipeline crosses tundra.

Building the pipeline created more interest in tundra and more environmental controversy than anything previously done in the North. Teams of scientists went to the Arctic to study the tundra, the wildlife and the effects of possible oil spills.

One of the major concerns was for the caribou. The

pipeline crosses caribou migration routes, and it was unclear how the animals would react to the structure. About half of the pipeline sits on low pilings just above the tundra. In places where caribou were likely to cross, the pipeline was buried. If that wasn't possible, the pipeline was elevated to allow the caribou to go underneath.

The pipeline was finished in 1977, but it is still not known what the long-range effects on the caribou will be. So far, winter migrations have not been seriously affected, but in the spring, cows and calves avoid the pipeline and the oilfields. Tundra caribou are easily frightened, but it doesn't seem to be the pipeline itself that makes the herds shy away. Rather it is the truck traffic on the road alongside the pipeline. Wild animals are especially wary of anything that moves.

An intrusion in the wilderness, like the building of a road or pipeline, always effects wildlife. In Alaska, it also stirred heated debate. Some people argued the Arctic was just a frozen wasteland, and oil was more important than plants or animals. Others talked about the fragile tundra, and how the environment must be protected against development. They said we waste too much oil already.

These arguments are not easy to resolve. Oil is important, but the caribou were there long before the drilling rigs were set up and the pipeline started pumping oil.

Can we have both oil and caribou from the tundra? Perhaps, but only if we are very careful. Much will be learned by watching the situation in Alaska.

For the Eskimos of northern Alaska, the oil brought money, but problems too. Millions of dollars in land settlement claims were paid to villages that had been quite poor. With this money they built schools and improved their towns. Older people who had once lived in sod shelters now had houses with running water.

But money isn't everything, especially to a people whose life had once centered around hunting whales. Now, suddenly, they were faced with a new way of life that was very different from the old. Jobs began to replace hunting and time was measured with clocks instead of the movement of the sun and the stars. This disruption of the old ways of life led to an increase in alcoholism in many communities.

Few people in the past have faced such rapid change, but in Alaska native people are learning how to solve their problems and adjust to the new ways. Basketball, played in warm gymnasiums, has already become a favorite sport on the North Slope.

The Canadian Eskimos call themselves *Inuit,* which means, the people. Eskimo is an Indian word, from south of the treeline, meaning one who eats raw meat.

The Inuit were once a nomadic people, moving from camp to camp, wherever the hunting and fishing were best. They were the only Arctic natives who actually lived in igloos during the winter. Life for the Inuit was always a struggle. Many of them suffered greatly when the caribou herds declined.

Today the Inuit live in villages built by the Canadian government in the 1960s. Prefabricated houses were brought in by ship and set up on the tundra. The villages resemble tiny suburban developments. Most of them are on the coast near former hunting camps.

The Inuit are still in the process of transition between the old ways and the new. Hunting and fishing are important sources of food for them, but ice cream, spaghetti, and bubble gum are available at the store. Men and women who were born in igloos by the light of a seal oil lamp, now spend their evenings watching programs beamed in by satellite television. For some Inuit, the only trees they have ever seen are the pines flown in at Christmas.

Inuit children attend grade schools in their villages. The classes are taught mostly in English, although a native language may be spoken at home. Most of the villages are very small, under a thousand people, and have no high school. If boys or girls want to get high school educations, they must leave their villages and fly to boarding schools far away. Many Inuit do not go.

The Inuit land, including the barren lands, is largely undeveloped. This means better hunting and fishing, but few jobs for the people. Some have turned to arts and crafts to earn money. The Inuit are well known for their

skillful carvings in stone and ivory. Each village also welcomes tourists with a tiny hotel.

The Inuit, and the other Arctic natives, have endured the uncertainties of northern life for many, many generations. If asked why they stay in the North, a person born on the tundra may speak of the beauty of the hills or the long summer days. But more often they will just smile and say, "It is my home."

The barren lands are almost untouched by people. Circles of stones still mark places where hunters pitched their tents long ago. A few fishing camps now operate in the summer. A trapper may have an isolated cabin, but there is no junk in rivers and never a piece of litter along the bank. The water is pure enough to drink without treatment.

Yet even the barren lands may change. Twice I saw

tall wooden stakes on the tundra, although the nearest settlements were weeks away by canoe. The stakes marked claims of prospectors looking for uranium ore. Would there be a mine there someday, and perhaps a town? If so, would the river still be clean enough to drink? And what would become of the animals?

These were questions that came to mind, paddling through the silence of the tundra afternoons.

Chapter 9

Autumn Returns

S UMMER was ending on the tundra as we reached our last campsite. The bearberry leaves were turning scarlet, although August had just begun. A strong south wind had pushed us on all day, but the sky was overcast and heavy. It was unusually warm and we had paddled the last stretch of river in tee shirts. The hills of the last few days were lost in the distance as the ground became flat again.

We pulled up against a stony beach and unstrapped the packs from the canoes. The food packs were light now, for almost everything had been eaten. We carried the canoes up the bank and turned them over.

Our campsite was at the edge of a broad plain. It was nearly level and spongy with water. The tents were pitched over the lumpy high spots, the driest land around. A few flowers still bloomed, but most were gone, their brown seeds scattered in the tundra grass. In the distance, beyond the wet meadow, a pair of lakes formed

120

silver lines against a stony landscape. I walked far out on the tundra that evening, but the tents were still visible as little specks of orange and green.

I awoke early the next day. The wind had shifted to the north and was rattling the tent. Clouds hurried across a bright sky. It was cold, but still above freezing. I put on a turtle neck, a shirt, a heavy sweater, a down vest, a wind parka, a wool hat and gloves and went for a walk. As I gathered bilberries, the strong wind blew them from my hand.

After breakfast we packed and waited for the plane to come. Alex had radioed our position to the pilot the day before. The wind continued, and as we stood around, I began to wish I had put on long underwear too.

The plane arrived suddenly. It skimmed the bank, dropped down to the river, and landed on the choppy water. When it taxied to shore, we tied the pontoons to the boulders on the beach and began loading our gear.

In my pack were a few souvenirs, a bit of caribou fur, a little piece of antler, a snowy owl feather and a tuft of qiviut.

When everything was carefully stowed away, we climbed in through the low door. I cinched my seat belt tight as the pilot brought the engines up to a full whining roar. The plane raced across the river, straight for the bank, then lifted free and soared above the tundra. I settled down by the window for the long flight back.

Behind us, on the tundra, the animals were preparing for another winter. The twilight of the Arctic nights was growing dim, and soon darkness would return to the North. Throughout the tundra, the cranberries were ripening as the first frost neared.

In August, the birds sense the shortening of the days. Then the Arctic terns give up their place on the river and find the way to the sea. By the time the first snow settles on the lichen, the terns will be gone, following the sun southward.

For the animals that remain behind, autumn is the last chance to eat well before winter. Now, an Arctic fox may catch a few fat ground squirrels before they begin hibernating. Once the land freezes, the ground squirrels will be safe from predators until spring.

The caribou move southward as the snows come, and the wolves follow. A silence falls on the tundra. Often, the only noise is the wind. It plays over the hills and sends ripples across the ponds until they too, are frozen and still.

Autumn ends when the deep cold comes down from the North Pole. Then the muskoxen band together on the hills, and the snowy owls search the plains for lemmings.

As the cold settles on the land, the sun dips lower in the sky. Before it leaves the tundra, the sun lingers for a while on the southern horizon. Sunrise, high noon, and sunset, all take place at once. For a moment the rocks and white hills are washed with red, pink, and yellow light. Blades of dead grass cast long shadows as they swing back and forth. Then the color and the sun are gone.

In winter the Arctic is a place of black and white. The sky is a luminous dark and even the lakes disappear under the smooth whiteness of the snow. Until the sun returns again, the tundra is a cold, forbidding, and unbelievably desolate land.

GLOSSARY

Alder-a woody shrub of the birch family

Arctic-the northern region of the world (the word comes from Arktos, meaning bear, which refers to the polar constellation Ursa Major, the big dipper)

Cache-to store or hide

Camouflage-coloring that blends in with the surroundings

Carbohydrate-a plant compound (like starch) that is related to sugar

Chlorophyll-a green compound found in plant leaves that converts carbon dioxide and water to sugar in the presence of light

Dormant-temporarily inactive

Fellfield-a field of rocks

Inushuk-chunks of rock stacked to resemble a person

Jaeger-a dark, gull-like bird

Lichen-a primitive plant that often grows on rocks

Migrate-travel to a different place with the seasons

Muskox-a bisonlike animal of the Arctic

Northern lights-glowing streams of light that appear in the upper atmosphere of the northern sky

Permafrost-ground that is always frozen

Pontoon-the float of an airplane that lands on water

Predator-a hunting animal

Ptarmigan-a northern grouselike bird with feathered feet

Qiviut-underfur of the muskox

Regurgitate-to throw up

Scavenger-an animal that feeds on dead animals

Starch-a plant food related to sugar

Taiga-a Russian word for the northern forest

Tamarack-a tree that resembles a fir, but sheds all its needles each fall

Tundra-the treeless plain of the Arctic (a Russian-Finnish word)

BIBLIOGRAPHY

*indicates books for younger readers

Anderson, Sally. "Norway's Reindeer Lapps." *National
Geographic,* vol. 152, no. 3, pp. 364-379 (Sept. 1977).

*Barry, Scott. *The Kingdom of Wolves.* G. P. Putnam's Sons, 1979,
New York.

Bland, John H. *Forests of Lilliput: the Realm of Mosses and
Lichens.* Prentice-Hall, 1971, Englewood Cliffs, NJ.

Brummer, Fred. *The Arctic,* Quadrangle, 1973,
New York.

Chadwick, Douglas H. "Our Wildest Wilderness," *National
Geographic,* vol. 156, no. 6, pp. 737-769, (Dec. 1979).

*Fox, Michael W. *The Wolf.* Coward, Mccann & Geoghegan, 1973,
New York.

*Goetz, Delia. *The Arctic Tundra.* William Morrow & Co., 1958,
New York.

*Harrington, Lyn. *The Polar Regions.* Thomas Nelson, 1973,
Nashville, TN.

Hodgson, Bryan. "The Pipeline: Alaska's Troubled Colossus,"
National Geographic, vol. 150, no. 5, pp. 684-717 (Nov. 1976).

*Hopf, Alice L. *Biography of a Snowy Owl.* G. P. Putnam's Sons,
1979, New York.

*Hunt, Patricia. *Snowy Owls.* Dodd, Mead & Co., 1982, New York.

Irving, L. *Arctic Life of Birds and Mammals.* Springer-Verlag, 1972, New York.

Ives, Jack D. and Barry, Roger G., Editors. *Arctic and Alpine Environments.* Methuen & Co., 1972, London.

*Laycock, George. *Beyond the Arctic Circle.* Four Winds Press, 1978, New York.

Lopez, Barry Holstun. *Of Wolves and Men.* Charles Scribner's Sons, 1978, New York.

Lvov, Anatoli. "Norilsk, Where is That?" *Soviet Life,* no. 2 (329), pp. 42-47 (Feb. 1984).

Mowat, Farley. *Never Cry Wolf.* Little, Brown & Co., 1963, Boston. *People of the Deer.* McClelland & Stewart, 1975, Toronto. *The Siberians.* Atlantic-Little Brown, 1970, Boston.

Pruitt, William O., Jr. *Animals of the North.* Harper & Row, 1967, New York.

*Rau, Margaret. *Musk Oxen.* Crowell, 1976, New York.

Rearden, Jim. "Caribou: Hardy Nomads of the North," *National Geographic,* vol. 146, no. 6, pp. 858-878 (Dec. 1974).

Remmert, Hermann. *Arctic Animal Ecology,* Springer-Verlag, 1980, New York.

Resnick, Abraham. *Siberia and the Soviet Far East: Endless Frontiers.* Novosti Press Agency, 1983, Moscow.

Rytkheu, Yuri. "People of the Long Spring," *National Geographic,* vol. 163, no. 2, pp. 206-223 (Feb. 1983).

Seton, Ernest Thompson. *Arctic Prairies.* International University Press, 1911, New York.

Tieszen, Larry L., Editor. *Vegetation and Production Ecology of an Alaskan Arctic Tundra,* Springer-Verlag, 1978, New York.

Vesilind, Priit J. "Hunters of the Lost Spirit," *National Geographic,* vol. 163, no. 2, pp. 151-196 (Feb. 1983).

Zahl, Paul A. "Portrait of a Fierce and Fragile Land," *National Geographic,* vol. 141, no. 3, pp. 303-337 (March 1972).

INDEX